THIS BOOK BELONGS TO:

_____

This edition published in Great Britain in 1997 by
PAVILION BOOKS LIMITED
London House, Great Eastern Wharf, Parkgate Road, London SW11 4NQ

Text © Nicola Moon 1995
Illustrations copyright © Anthony Morris 1995

The moral right of the author and illustrator
has been asserted.

Designed by Peter Sims/Linda Rogers Associates

A CIP catalogue record for this book is available
from the British Library.

ISBN 18205 077 5

Printed in Singapore by Khai Wah Ferco

2 4 6 8 10 8 7 5 3

This book can be ordered direct from the publisher. Please contact
the Marketing Department. But try your bookshop first.

Mouse Finds a Seed

Nicola Moon
Illustrated by Anthony Morris

PAVILION

One day, Mouse found a seed.
'What is it ?' he asked Mole.
'It's a seed,' said Mole.
'It grows into a flower.'
'When ?' asked Mouse.
'When it's ready,' said Mole.

Mouse put the seed beside his bed. In the morning, he said to Mother Mouse, 'My seed won't grow.'

'It needs to be in the earth,'
Mother Mouse told him.
So Mouse planted the seed
in a bowl of earth.

Later that day, he said to Frog,
'My seed won't grow.'
'It needs water,' Frog advised.
So Mouse gave his seed some
water.

After lunch he said to Rabbit, 'My seed still won't grow.' 'Perhaps it's cold,' Rabbit suggested. So Mouse put the bowl with his seed in the warm sunshine.

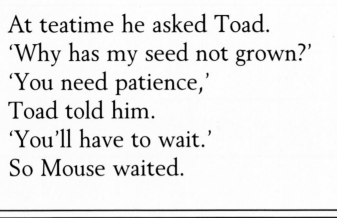

At teatime he asked Toad.
'Why has my seed not grown?'
'You need patience,'
Toad told him.
'You'll have to wait.'
So Mouse waited.

Every day he looked at the damp earth in his bowl. For a long time nothing happened. But he kept the earth damp and he kept it warm. And he waited...

...for days, and days, and days...
and one day, when he couldn't
bear to wait any longer, there it
was...

... a tiny, green, straight
and pointy shoot!

'It's growing,' Mouse told Mole.
'It's growing,' he told Frog and
Rabbit and Toad. 'What shall I do
now?' he asked Mother Mouse.
'You must look after it very
carefully,' Mother Mouse said.
So Mouse looked after his shoot.

He watered it every day. He sheltered it from the wind and the fierce sun. He protected it from snails and caterpillars. He even talked to it.
Mouse watched the shoot grow big and strong.

He watched the leaves spread
out and reach towards the sky.
But most of all he watched the
big fat round bud that grew at
the top of the stem.

'It's beautiful!' said Mole.
'It's magnificent!' said Frog.
'It's very tall!' said Toad.
'It's just like the sun,'
said Rabbit.
'It's a SUNFLOWER!'
said Mother Mouse.
'It's mine!' said Mouse.
'I grew it from a seed.'

And then, one day...